E
P

Pearson, Susan

Saturday I ran away

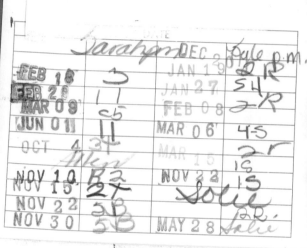

water damage
noted 2/3/87

SATURDAY I RAN AWAY

SATURDAY I RAN AWAY

Susan Pearson

illustrated by

Susan Jeschke

J.B. LIPPINCOTT
New York

I hate being the littlest! Like last night. Katy and I were setting the table. Katy is my big sister. She dropped a glass.

Mom heard it break. "What was that, girls?" she said.

"Emily broke a glass," said Katy.

"I did not!" I said. "I was setting the silverware. Forks don't break!"

"It's all right, Emily," said Mom. "Just clean it up."

That Katy. She blames everything on me!

At dinner, Dad said, "Why the long face, Emily?"

"She broke a glass," said Katy.

"I did not!" I yelled.

"No yelling at the table," said Dad.

After dinner I had to go to the bathroom. It took awhile. Dad knocked on the door.

"Emily," he said. "Come out right this minute. No one has to go this soon after eating. You haven't had time to digest your food yet. You're just trying to get out of helping with the dishes."

I was not. I really did have to go. Can I help it if
I digest fast? Maybe it was lunch.

Next I wanted to play Moonlight–Starlight. That's a game. You play it outside. It's kind of like hide-and-seek. But you play it after dark. It's real spooky.

All the kids play after supper. Tom was already playing. He's my big brother.

"Can I go play?" I asked Mom.

"Sure," she said. "But don't go wandering off. You know the boundaries."

I went outside.

"What do you think you're doing?" said Tom.

"I want to play," I said. "Mom said I could."

"Well, I say you can't," said Tom. "You're too little. You just get scared."

"I can play if I want to," I said.

But Tom said, "We're going to play at Roger's house." I can't go that far after dark. Tom knows it, too.

That's when I decided to run away. They'll be sorry. They'll miss me.

First I made a list of what I'd need:
    peanut butter and marshmallow sandwiches
    ants on a log
    bug juice
    blanket
    books
    flashlight

"What's this?" Mom asked me.

"It's a list," I said.

"I can see that," said Mom. "What's it a list of?"

"The things I'll need," I told her. "For running away."

"When are you going?" she asked.

"Tomorrow," I said.

"You're lucky," she said.

"I am?"

"I wish I could run away sometimes," she said.

I was kind of surprised.

This morning I was fixing ants on a log. First you spread peanut butter on celery. Then you stick raisins into the peanut butter. Get it? The celery is the log. The raisins are the ants. Neat, huh?

I was wrapping them in waxed paper. Tom came in.

"Whatcha doin'?" he asked.

"Packing a lunch," I said.

"I can see that," he said. "What for?"

"I'm running away," I told him.

"Good idea," he said.

"Creep," I called him.

"I didn't mean it mean," Tom said. "I just meant I wish I could run away."

"Well, can't you?" I asked.

"No way," he said. "If I miss that test on Monday, Mrs. Burns will flunk me in geography. And if I flunk geography, I'll miss the game on Friday because Dad'll ground me. He's really on my case about grades."

He fixed himself a sandwich and went back outside. I made some bug juice. That's Kool-Aid.

"Looks good," said Dad. "Can I have a glass?"

"Just a little one," I told him. "I need most of it. I'm running away."

"Really?" he said. "I remember when I ran away. I was just about your age. I took the flatboat up the river a piece and fished all day. It was swell. I sure wish I could do that now. Just disappear for a day." He sighed. "Oh, well. Have a good time. And thanks for the bug juice."

I went to my bedroom to pack my bag. Katy came in. There's no way to keep her out. We share the room.

She looked at the bag on my bed.

"What are *you* doing?" she asked.

"Nothing," I said.

"Running away?" she asked.

"Who told?"

"Nobody," she said. "I just figured you would, sooner or later. I would, too, if I weren't too old for that. I'd sure like to get away from that brat Tom for a while. He's driving me nuts." She took a book from the bookcase and left.

I sat down on my bed. It looked like my whole family wanted to run away. I needed to think about that.

All of a sudden I had an idea. First I'd need to pack a few more things. I put in my frisbee, and Katy's drawing pad and pencils, and the thick book Mom was in the middle of. Then I wrote a note:

TO THE PERSON IN THIS FAMILY WHO WISHED HE OR SHE COULD RUN AWAY THIS MORN-ING—I NEED YOUR HELP. PLEASE MEET ME AT THE BEND IN THE CREEK UNDER THE SWING-ING TREE. YOU DON'T HAVE TO STAY.

EMILY

I stuck the note to the refrigerator door. Then I got Dad's fishing pole from the garage and left.

I spread my blanket out under the tree and waited. It wasn't long until Tom came along. He was carrying his fishing pole and a tin can full of bait.

"What's the matter?" he asked. I just stared at his fishing pole. He shrugged. "I figured I might as well bring it along."

"I won't need your help for a little while," I told him. "Can you wait?"

"I guess so," said Tom. "I'll fish."

He slid down the bank and got started right away.

Pretty soon I saw Katy coming. Tom couldn't see her, but she saw Tom.

"What's *he* doing here?" she asked.

"You'll see in a little while," I told her. "Can you wait a few minutes? You can draw while you're waiting." I handed her the pad and pencils.

Katy looked suspicious. "I don't know what you're up to, Emily," she said. "But as long as *he's* down there and I'm up here, I guess I can wait to find out." She sat down under the tree and began to draw.

In about ten minutes, along came Dad. "What is this, a convention?" he said.

"Sort of," I said. "You'll see in a couple more minutes."

He spotted his fishing pole. "Meanwhile, I can fish, right?"

He slid down the bank to where Tom was already fishing.

A couple minutes later, there was Mom. She looked at me. Then she looked at Tom and Dad down by the creek. Then she looked at Katy. Katy looked at her. They started to laugh.

Tom and Dad heard them and came up the bank.

"What's going on?" said Dad. Then he looked at Katy and Mom and he started to laugh, too.

Tom scratched his head. "You mean all of us are THE PERSON IN THIS FAMILY WHO WISHED HE COULD RUN AWAY?" he asked.

"Or she," I said.

"You know, Emily," he said, "for a little kid, you're pretty tricky." And he started to laugh, too.

We stayed at the creek all day long, drawing and fishing and reading and playing frisbee and swinging on the swinging tree. When it began to get dark, we started home.

"I'll fry these fish for supper," said Dad. "Mmmm."

"What a nice day," said Katy. She sounded sort of surprised.

"Yeah, it was," said Tom. He sounded even more surprised.

"I guess we all learned a lesson today," said Mom. "We won't forget it. Thank you, Emily."

"It's nothing," I said.

I guess the lesson she meant was that we should be nicer to one another so that everybody doesn't want to run away. But she's wrong about not forgetting it. They all will. Probably by tomorrow. I know that. But there's one thing *I'll* never forget. "Pretty tricky" is the nicest thing Tom has ever called me.

Library of Congress Cataloging in Publication Data
Pearson, Susan.
    Saturday I ran away.
    Summary: Emily runs away from home and helps the
rest of her family join her.
    [1. Runaways—Fiction] I. Jeschke, Susan. II. Title.
PZ7.P323316Sat 1981   [E]   81-47107
ISBN 0-397-31957-6
ISBN 0-397-31958-4 (lib. bdg.)

1   2   3   4   5   6   7   8   9   10

First Edition